Princess Mirror-Belle

and the Sea Monster's Cave

★ JULIA DONALDSON ★

Princess Mirror-Belle

and the Sea Monster's Cave

Illustrated by
LYDIA MONKS

MACMILLAN CHILDREN'S BOOKS

These stories first published 2006 in *Princess Mirror-Belle and the Flying Horse*
by Macmillan Children's Books

This edition published 2015 by Macmillan Children's Books
an imprint of Pan Macmillan
20 New Wharf Road, London N1 9RR
Associated companies throughout the world
www.panmacmillan.com

ISBN 978-1-4472-8566-3

1 3 5 7 9 8 6 4 2

A CIP catalogue record for this book is available from
the British Library.

Printed and bound by CPI Group (UK) Ltd, Croydon CR0 4YY

For Gaby

Contents

Chapter One

The Sea Monster's Cave

"For goodness sake," said Ellen impatiently to her big brother, who was pushing yet another coin into his favourite seaside slot machine. "I bet Granny and Grandpa wouldn't want you to waste all their money on that thing."

"I'm not wasting it. I'm going to end up with more than I started with." Luke's teeth were gritted and his eyes had a determined gleam. "Can't you see, that

whole pile of coins is about to tumble off the edge. Then I'll win them all! I'll probably win them next go." But he didn't; or the next go or the one after that.

They had been on holiday for a week, staying in a caravan park with their grandparents. Granny and Grandpa had gone out for a last row in their boat and had given Luke and Ellen ten pounds spending money each.

"I'm sick of hanging around waiting for you," Ellen complained. "At this rate I won't get to the shops at all. Don't forget, they're taking us out this afternoon, and tomorrow we're going home."

"Well, why don't I see you back here in an hour," suggested Luke, and Ellen agreed, even though she knew he had promised to look after her.

There were two gift shops by the beach. Ellen wandered round one of them and chose a packet of sparkly pens and a little notepad with a picture of a seal and "Best wishes from Whitesands" on the front. She paid for them and put them in her backpack, along with her sun lotion.

She still had six pounds left so she went into the second shop, which sold all sorts of ornamental sea creatures – fish, lobsters and sea horses – as well as boxes covered in shiny shells. Most things were too expensive, but Ellen enjoyed looking round. Tucked away in a corner she found a beautiful

mirror decorated
round the outside
with a mermaid and
shells. It cost £9.99,
and Ellen began
to wish she hadn't
bought the things in
the first shop. She

was just wondering whether she could take
them back when a voice from the mermaid
mirror said, "So it *is* you! I nearly didn't
recognize you under all those freckles." It
was Princess Mirror-Belle.

"Mirror-Belle!" Ellen hadn't seen her
mirror friend all holidays and felt quite
pleased to see her now, even though she
knew there was bound to be trouble ahead.
"You've got lots of freckles too," she said.

"Don't be silly – they're not freckles, they're beauty spots," replied Princess Mirror-Belle, and she dived out of the mirror, landing on her hands with her legs in the air.

The shop assistant must have heard the thud. She left the customer she was serving and hurried over to them, looking cross.

"Please don't do hand-stands in here," she said to Mirror-Belle. "You might break something."

"It wasn't a handstand. It was a dive," said Mirror-Belle, on her feet by now.

"With all these sea creatures around, I naturally assumed I would land in the sea. It's extremely confusing; I suggest you remove them and put some land animals on the shelves instead."

"Why don't you go and play on the beach?" said the shop assistant.

"I didn't hear you say, 'Your Royal Highness'," objected Mirror-Belle, "but it's quite a good idea, so I'll excuse you just this once. Come on, Ellen."

"Sorry," Ellen murmured to the assistant, and she followed Mirror-Belle out of the shop and on to the beach.

Three children were digging in the sand. Mirror-Belle went up to them.

"I doubt if you'll find any treasure here," she said. "The sea monster is much

more likely to have hidden it in a cave, and
he's probably guarding it."

The children just stared at her.
"They're not digging for treasure –
they're building a sandcastle," Ellen told
Mirror-Belle.

"What a ridiculous idea! You can't build a castle out of sand. I should know, I live in one."

"I thought you lived in a palace," said Ellen.

"That's in the winter. In the summer we go to our castle by the sea. It's made of pure white marble with ivory towers." Mirror-Belle turned back to the children. "In any case, you shouldn't build it on the beach. Don't you realize it will collapse when the tide comes in?"

"We don't mind," said one of them. "We'll have gone home by then."

"What? You're building a castle and you're not even going to live in it?" Mirror-Belle shook her head pityingly. "There's no hope for them, Ellen. We'd better move on," she said.

"Shall we look for shells?" suggested Ellen as they walked along between the sea and the row of beach umbrellas.

Instead of answering her, Mirror-Belle gazed at the sky and then marched up to the nearest umbrella. A man and a woman were dozing underneath it.

"Allow me," said Mirror-Belle, and she stepped over them and closed the umbrella.

"Hey, what are you doing?"

said the woman, sitting up.

"What does it look like?" answered Mirror-Belle. "There's not a trace of rain, so you really don't need an umbrella."

The man was on his feet by this time. "Buzz off," he said as he opened the umbrella up again.

"I'm a princess, not a bee," replied Mirror-Belle.

Ellen tugged at her arm and Mirror-Belle allowed herself to be pulled away, but not without saying in a loud voice, "I'm beginning to wonder if this is a special beach for idiots."

"They're not idiots," Ellen told her off when they were out of earshot. "They just don't want to get sunburned. That reminds me, I ought to put some lotion on." She took the bottle out of her back-pack. "It's to protect me against the sun," she explained, and then realized that Mirror-Belle had an identical bag on her back. "Haven't you got some too?"

"Not exactly," said Mirror-Belle, opening her own bag. Ellen looked inside and saw some sparkly pens and a notepad just like the ones she had just bought. Mirror-Belle took out a bottle and unscrewed the cap. "This is to protect me against sea monsters," she said as she smeared some of it over her neck and arms.

Ellen laughed. "I don't

think you get sea monsters in Whitesands," she said.

"I wouldn't be so sure," replied Mirror-Belle darkly. She screwed up her eyes and looked out to sea. "I can't see any," she admitted, "though I can see some rather ugly mermaids on that rock. Their tails look all right, but why haven't they got long golden hair?"

Ellen looked too and laughed again. "Those aren't mermaids – they're seals," she said.

"Well, give me mermaids any day," replied Mirror-Belle. "The rocks near our castle are covered in them."

"Do you play with them?" asked Ellen, though she wasn't really sure if she believed in these mermaids.

"Sometimes. It's not much fun though, because they spend so much time combing their hair." Mirror-Belle paused for a moment and then added, "One of them gave me a magic comb for my birthday."

"What was magic about it?" asked Ellen.

"It could change your hair into any style you wished for. The colour too. I once had purple ringlets down to my toes."

"Have you still got the comb?"

"Really, Ellen, I wish you wouldn't always ask so many questions. If you must know, it was stolen by a sea monster."

"Are sea monsters hairy then?"

"Of course. I thought even you would know that."

They reached the rocky end of the beach, where there were fewer people. They picked seaweed off the rocks and made necklaces with it and a crown for Mirror-Belle, who said, "It's a shame you can't have one too, Ellen, but the only way you could become a princess would be to marry a prince."

They wandered along the curved shore further than Ellen had ever been before. There were cliffs behind them now and they had to clamber over boulders. They reached the tip of the bay and carried on into the next one.

"Look!" said Mirror-Belle, pointing to an opening at the foot of a cliff. "That's the entrance to a cave. I wonder if it belongs to the sea monster. Would you like some of my protective lotion, Ellen?"

"All right," said Ellen, just to keep Mirror-Belle happy. She was pretty sure that sea monsters didn't exist; at least, they might do in Mirror-Belle's world, but not here in Whitesands.

The cave, when they reached it, was disappointing. It was quite small and empty, except for a couple of cans and a lemonade bottle. "No sign of any sea monster," said Ellen.

"On the contrary." Mirror-Belle had picked up the empty lemonade bottle and was looking excited. "Didn't you know, they love lemonade? If they don't drink lots of it, they lose their slime."

"I thought you said they were hairy," Ellen objected, but Mirror-Belle didn't seem to have heard her. She was examining some writing on the wall of the cave. Ellen looked too and saw that a lot of people had carved their names into the rock. "Look at this!" said Mirror-Belle, pointing to some rather wiggly letters which said: "T. Box 1.8.01."

"What about it?" asked Ellen.

"Can't you see? It's a clue. The 'T' must stand for treasure."

"It probably stands for Tom or Tessa or

something," said Ellen. "And Box is their surname."

"The poor creature has written it back to front," Mirror-Belle carried on, ignoring

Ellen, "but then sea monsters aren't very intelligent. Never mind – look at those numbers, Ellen: they're the important thing. They show us where the treasure box is buried."

"I think they're just the date," said Ellen. "'1.8.01' means the first of August, 2001. That's when this Box person carved their name."

"Nothing of the sort," scoffed Mirror-Belle. "It means that we have to take one step in one direction, eight steps in another direction and then dig one foot underground."

Ellen frowned doubtfully. This wasn't the first time Mirror-Belle had been so excited about treasure. Ellen remembered when she had claimed that her dog, Prince

Precious Paws, could sniff out gold and jewels, but he hadn't succeeded.

"Don't look so gloomy, Ellen," Mirror-Belle reproached her. "You should be even happier than I am! After all, I'm incredibly rich already, but think what a difference all this wealth will make to you."

This reminded Ellen of Luke and all the coins in the slot machine.

"Help!" she said. "I must go. Luke will be getting worried – and I expect Granny and Grandpa will be back by now. Are you coming?"

"Of course not. Can't you see, this is the perfect opportunity to dig up the treasure, when the sea monster isn't guarding it."

"Do be careful, Mirror-Belle," said Ellen and then had to remind herself that sea monsters didn't really exist.

"Oh, I'll be fine. I've got my protective lotion, remember. But I'm surprised that you're leaving me to do all the digging by myself. Just think – there might even be a magic comb buried with all the gold and jewels. You'd like that, wouldn't you?"

But Ellen couldn't be persuaded. She hurried back over the rocks and along the beach. She found Luke pacing about outside the arcade of slot machines.

"Thank goodness you're back," he said. "They'd go mad if I'd lost you."

"Sorry," said Ellen. "I've been with Mirror-Belle."

"Oh, do shut up blaming everything on someone who doesn't even exist," Luke snapped at her. Ellen decided that now wasn't the best moment to ask him if he'd won any money, but from the expression on his face she doubted it.

That afternoon Granny and Grandpa took them out to a bird sanctuary, and they all had supper in a cafe on the way home.

"You're very quiet, Ellen, pet," said Granny.

"She's tired," said

Grandpa, but it wasn't that. Ellen couldn't help thinking about Mirror-Belle and hoping she was all right. Was she still in the cave or had she returned to her own world? Ellen half expected to find her waiting for them when they got back to the camper van, but she wasn't.

"Early to bed and early to rise," said Granny after the game of cards they always played in the evening. "We've got a long journey tomorrow."

But Ellen couldn't sleep. She lay awake in the camper van listening to her grandparents' gentle snores and worrying about Mirror-Belle. If only there was someone she could talk to! She wondered if Luke was still awake. He didn't sleep in the camper van but in a tent just outside.

Ellen put her anorak on over her pyjamas and slipped on her flip-flops. Quietly she opened the door of the camper van and stepped outside. It was a clear night and the moon was nearly full.

"Luke!" she whispered. She unzipped his tent a few inches and whispered again. There was no reply. Ellen knew he would only be cross if she woke him. She really should go back to bed, but instead she found herself walking down to the little beach where

Granny and Grandpa moored their rowing boat.

She looked out to sea. She could see the cliffs at the end of the bay, but now the tide was high, covering the boulders where she and Mirror-Belle had clambered that morning.

The next bay, the one with the cave, must be cut off by the tide. If Mirror-Belle was still there, she would be trapped. Usually she escaped into her own world through a mirror, but there wasn't one in the cave.

A breeze blew in from the sea and Ellen shivered. She thought of Mirror-Belle with no anorak to keep her warm. She wouldn't have had anything to eat either. And if she really did believe in sea monsters, she might be feeling scared as well as cold and hungry.

Then Ellen noticed something bobbing in the water. It was a plastic lemonade bottle. It looked as if there was something inside it: a scrap of paper.

Ellen rolled up her pyjama trousers, took a couple of steps into the cold water and reached out for the bottle. She unscrewed the top. Sure enough, there was a rolled-up piece of paper inside it. When Ellen unrolled it and saw the glittery backwards writing she knew at once who the message was from. This is what it said:

HELP! I AM TRAPPED IN THE SEA
MONSTER'S CAVE. I NEED A NICE PRINCE
TO RESCUE ME. THE REWARD WILL BE HALF
MY FATHER'S KINGDOM AND MY HAND IN
MARRIAGE (WHEN I AM OLD ENOUGH).

PRINCESS MIRROR-BELLE
XXX

Ellen was very good at reading backwards writing after all her adventures with Mirror-Belle, so she read it as:

HELP! I AM TRAPPED IN THE SEA
MONSTER'S CAVE. I NEED A NICE PRINCE
TO RESCUE ME. THE REWARD WILL BE HALF
MY FATHER'S KINGDOM AND MY HAND IN
MARRIAGE (WHEN I AM OLD ENOUGH).

PRINCESS MIRROR-BELLE
XXX

*

An hour later, Ellen and Luke were in their grandparents' boat. Luke was rowing. "This had better not be a trick," he said.

It had been easier than Ellen had imagined to wake her brother and talk him into this night-time rescue operation. Luke had always liked adventures, and although he had never before believed in Mirror-Belle, the back-to-front note in the bottle had seemed to convince him.

"There's the cave!" Ellen pointed at the dark hole in the cliff face. She was relieved to see that there was a strip of sand in front of the cave; at least it wasn't flooded.

"Look!" She stood up and pointed again in great excitement.

"Sit down – you're rocking the boat," said Luke. He was rowing with his back to the cliffs and couldn't see what Ellen could see – a pale figure standing in the mouth of the cave.

"Mirror-Belle!" she called out.

A few minutes later Mirror-Belle was climbing into the boat.

"Hello, Ellen," she said, and then, "My prince! My hero!" she greeted Luke.

"He's not a prince. He's just my brother," said Ellen.

"Never mind. He will be a prince once he marries me, won't you, my brave rescuer?" She flung her arms round Luke, who wriggled awkwardly out of her grasp. One of her seaweed necklaces had come off and stuck to him and he threw it into the sea.

"Settle down, you girls," he said, and picked up the oars.

"It's a pity you didn't get the chance to slay the sea monster," said Mirror-Belle. "I can't think where he can have got to."

Ellen was surprised that Mirror-Belle was in such a perky mood after being trapped in the cave for so long. "Did you find any treasure?" she asked.

But Mirror-Belle only seemed to want to talk to Luke. "Which half of my father's kingdom would you like?" she asked him as the boat bobbed along. "One half is covered in mountains and the other half is full of deep lakes."

Luke didn't reply but Mirror-Belle was not put out. She picked up the lemonade bottle with the note in it from the floor of the boat. "My father might ask a few questions about you at first, but I'm sure

I can make him see reason if I show him this," she said.

Ellen was beginning to feel annoyed. "It was me who found that, you know, not Luke. I've been worrying and worrying about you."

But Mirror-Belle's mind was still full of the marriage arrangements. "I suppose we'll have to wait about ten years," she said to Luke. "You could be learning a few princely things in the meantime, like hunting dragons and cutting off trolls' heads. Would you rather do that here or would you like to come back with me and have some lessons in the palace?"

"I'm trying to concentrate on the rowing," said Luke. Ellen could tell from his voice that he felt embarrassed.

"Luke doesn't want to get married," she told Mirror-Belle. "All he cares about is his band."

"That's not a problem," said Mirror-Belle. "He could be in a band of princes. They could be called the Dragon Slayers or the Royal Rescuers . . . or the Handsome Heroes." She turned back to Luke. "How would you like to play a golden guitar?"

"Am I just dreaming this?" Luke muttered.

They had reached the caravan park beach.

"I'll tie up the boat," said Luke as they clambered out. Mirror-Belle tried again to hug him, but he shrugged her off.

"Do you want to sleep in the camper van with me?" asked Ellen. "You'll have to be quiet, so as not to disturb Granny and Grandpa."

But Mirror-Belle didn't like this idea. "I'll sleep under the stars," she said. "Then I can guard my hero's tent in case the sea monster comes to take revenge."

"You'd better have my anorak then," said Ellen.

Luke offered rather reluctantly to sleep outside himself and let Mirror-Belle have the tent but she refused. "You've been enough of a hero for one night," she told him. "It's my turn to be a heroine."

"Your tea's cold," said Granny to Ellen the next morning. "I've tried to wake you about five times."

Ellen sat up in bed and noticed that Granny was holding her anorak.

"I found this on the ground outside," she said.

"Was Mirror-Belle there?" asked Ellen. "She said she wanted to sleep under the stars."

Granny chuckled. "That's some dream you've been having."

Grandpa came in. "That's it – I've fixed the boat to the tow bar," he said. "I was hoping that brother of yours would help me, but he's dead to the world."

"Shall we leave him behind, Ellen? What do you think?" joked Granny. But Ellen was thinking more about Mirror-Belle than about Luke. As soon as she was dressed she went outside to look for her. Luke was just staggering, bleary-eyed, out of his tent.

"Mirror-Belle seems to have gone," said Ellen. Luke looked blank for a second and then scratched his head. "That's funny – I had a dream about Mirror-Belle," he said. "Something about a message in a bottle and rescuing her in a boat."

"It wasn't a dream. It was real!" Ellen protested. "I can show you the bottle and the message!" But then she remembered that Mirror-Belle had them. By now she must have taken them back through some mirror or other into her own world.

Grandpa appeared at the doorway of the camper van. "Good afternoon," he said to Luke, though it was only half past nine. "You'd better start taking that tent down. Everything else is packed up."

He gave the windows of the camper van a loving wipe and then made a tut-tutting noise.

"What's the matter?" asked Luke.

"Someone's been fiddling about with the wing mirror. It's all bent back."

Grandpa straightened it out and then said, "That's funny."

"What is?" Ellen asked.

"There's seaweed all over it," said Grandpa. "I wonder how that got there?"

Ellen smiled to herself, but she said, "I can't think."

Chapter Two

The Unusual Pets Club

"Do you want to come back to my house for tea?" Ellen asked her best friend, Katy. They were in the school playground.

"I can't. I'm going to the Unusual Pets Club."

"What's that?"

"I don't really know much about it. It's the first meeting tonight, at Crystal's house. Hasn't she asked you too?"

"No." Ellen felt cross. Crystal was a

bossy girl in their class who was always starting up clubs and societies and then meanly not letting everyone join.

"You have to have an unusual pet to join it," said Katy. "Maybe you could bring Splodge along. Shall I ask Crystal?"

Ellen didn't know what to say. She wanted to pretend that she didn't care about the stupid old club, but in fact it sounded quite fun.

Just then, Crystal came up to them.

"Hi, Katy," she said. "Do you know how to get to my house?"

"I think so," said Katy. "Can Ellen come too?"

Crystal looked doubtful. "Well, I don't know. I didn't think you had an unusual pet, Ellen."

"She's got Splodge," said Katy. "He's a really nice dog. He's brilliant at chasing sticks and bringing them back, isn't he, Ellen?"

"But all dogs can do that," objected Crystal. "There's nothing unusual about it."

"What sort of unusual things do you mean?" asked Ellen. As far as she knew, Crystal's hamster, Silver, was perfectly normal.

But Crystal obviously didn't think so. "Well, like Silver, for instance," she said. "You know hamsters have two pouches in their cheeks and they stuff food in them? Well, Silver only ever uses his right pouch, never the left one – it's amazing!"

"And Twiglet can do this sort of dance," said Katy. Twiglet was her stick insect, and it was true that sometimes he moved from side to side in quite a rhythmic way, whereas most stick insects stayed still all the time.

"I tell you what, Ellen," said Crystal graciously. "See if you can teach Splodge a trick or something after school, and then you can bring him along at six o'clock. But it will be a sort of trial. If he's not unusual enough then he can't come to any of the other meetings."

When Ellen got home she found her old hula hoop and took Splodge out into the garden. She held the hoop out in front of him and said, "Jump!"

But Splodge didn't understand; he just

sat looking up at her eagerly as if he expected her to throw the hoop for him. Ellen had to give up on that trick.

She didn't succeed any better when she tried to teach Splodge to stand up and beg, or to thump his tail three times when she asked how old he was. The only thing he would do was shake hands, but Ellen didn't think Crystal would call that unusual enough.

A spider scuttled over Ellen's shoe and suddenly she had an idea. Her brother Luke had a pet tarantula called Evilton. A tarantula would surely

count as an unusual
pet.

She ran into the
house with Splodge
at her heels. Luke
was sprawled on the sofa watching
the music channel on television.

"Can I borrow Evilton?" asked Ellen
breathlessly.

"Be quiet – this is Fire Engine's new
release." Luke turned the volume up and
sang along with the band:

"So you think you can ride the storm,
    babe,
And there's nothing you can't do
But I can see a big wave coming
And it's gonna crash over you."

Ellen fidgeted impatiently till at last the song came to an end. Then she asked him again.

"Please, Luke. Just for this evening. I want to take him to the Unusual Pets Club."

"No," said Luke. "I'm not having Evilton join some silly girly club."

"It's not just for girls. Martin Booth is bringing his slow-worm. Oh, go on, Luke!"

"No," said Luke. "Evilton might catch cold. Anyway, I need him to help me with my homework!" He laughed as if this was hilarious, and when Ellen tried to argue he turned the volume up even louder. Fire Engine was singing another song.

Suddenly Ellen realized that she had missed most of her favourite programme,

Holiday Swap. She picked up the remote control, but Luke snatched it back.

"You're so mean," said Ellen. "This stuff is on twenty-four hours a day, and *Holiday Swap* only lasts half an hour."

"I got here first," said Luke, and he made her wait while the band was interviewed before he handed over the control. "OK – it's all yours," he said at last, and went out of the room, leaving the door open.

Ellen switched channels. *Holiday Swap* had just finished.

"I hate you," she shouted after Luke. She turned the television off angrily. Splodge laid his chin on her lap and she stroked his head. "You're the only nice one," she told him.

"What about me?" came a ghostly

whisper. The voice sounded slightly familiar, and for a moment Ellen wondered if it was Mirror-Belle. But there was no mirror in the room, and anyway the voice was too soft to be Mirror-Belle's.

Splodge had heard the mysterious whisper too, and he didn't like it. He whined and hid behind the sofa, leaving Ellen to stare at the television, which is where the voice seemed to have come from. And yet she had definitely turned it off – the screen was dull and blank. Actually, that wasn't quite true: Ellen could just see herself in it, but it wasn't what she would call a proper reflection; it was faint and grey and transparent.

"Happy Throughsday," whispered the faint grey transparent person, and stepped out of the television.

"Mirror-Belle – it is you! But you look all funny – like a ghost! I can see right through you."

"Well, what do you expect on Throughsday?" said Princess Mirror-Belle.

Her voice was a little louder now, more of an eerie chant than a whisper.

"You sound funny too. And what do you mean – Throughsday? It's Thursday today."

"It may be Thursday here, but back home it's Throughsday," said Mirror-Belle. "Everyone can walk through things on Throughsday. Like this." And she walked through the sofa. Splodge growled.

"That's amazing!" said Ellen. "Can you go through doors too?"

"Naturally, but someone seems to have left this one open."

"That's Luke. He's so irritating." Ellen closed the door and watched as Mirror-Belle glided through it and back again.

Splodge barked furiously.

"It's a pity you can't keep him under better control," said Mirror-Belle. "Still, I suppose I shouldn't expect your dog to be as well behaved as mine, seeing that he doesn't have any royal blood."

In fact, Mirror-Belle's dog, Prince Precious Paws, was the worst-behaved pet Ellen had ever met. She remembered the time he had stolen a roast chicken and scared a lot of sheep, but she decided not to mention this. Instead, now that they were on the subject of dogs, she found herself telling Mirror-Belle all about the Unusual Pets Club and how annoying Crystal was.

"And Luke's been horrible too," she said. "Everyone seems to be against me."

A thoughtful look crossed Mirror-Belle's

face. "I can change that," she said, and she walked through the television.

Splodge began to bark at the television as if this should have stopped Mirror-Belle.

"Calm down," Ellen told him, but Mirror-Belle said, "He needs to look at the television. It's part of the plan."

Just then, a strange echoey barking sound came from the screen.

"Here he comes, the dear sweet creature," Mirror-Belle said, and the next second a ghostly Prince Precious Paws bounded out of the screen and into the room.

"There's your unusual pet," said Mirror-Belle to Ellen. "At least, he's mine, really, but I'll let you borrow him."

Luke was hungry. Supper wouldn't be for ages: Mum was still teaching the piano. He opened the kitchen cupboard and found a jar of salsa.

"But I can see a big wave coming
   And it's gonna crash over you," he sang as he rummaged around some more. That Fire Engine song was so brilliant. Luke

wished he could write something as good as that for his own band, Breakneck.

He discovered a bag of rather stale crisps and dipped one into the bright red salsa. Suddenly he felt inspired. "Red, the colour of anger," he said to himself. That would be a good first line. How could the song go after that?

"Red, the colour of anger,

Blue, the colour of sorrow . . ." he sang with his mouth full. He was pausing to think what could come next, when a soft, eerie voice behind him sang:

"And green for the mean, mean brother

Who wouldn't let his sister borrow."

Luke looked over his shoulder and saw Ellen. At least, he thought he saw her, but the next second she had gone. She seemed to have disappeared through the wall. But of course she couldn't have done that.

"Ellen!" Luke strode out of the kitchen and into the television room. Only Splodge was there, sitting in front of the television and staring at the blank screen. Ellen was probably hiding somewhere, giggling. Oh well, he wouldn't give her the satisfaction of looking for her. Better make a start on his homework.

Up in his room, Luke found it hard to concentrate on the Second World War. He kept thinking about Ellen and feeling a bit guilty that he hadn't let her borrow his pet.

Evilton was burrowing about in the bark chippings inside his tank on Luke's table. As Luke watched him the words of a new song began to form themselves in his mind.

"You just want to poison me
But I'm not gonna let you start . . ."

He chewed his pen and wondcred how to carry on. Then his skin prickled as he heard the same ghostly voice as before.

"You just want to poison me
And I'm dying of a broken heart."

Luke jumped up and turned round. There stood Ellen, and yet he hadn't heard her come into the room.

"Ellen – why can't you knock

before you . . ." Luke's voice trailed off and
he stared at his sister. With a cold shock,
he realized he could see right through her.

"Ellen, what's the matter . . . you look
all . . . You look like a . . ." Luke couldn't
bring himself to say the word "ghost".

The ghostly girl gave a small sad smile.
"I forgive you," she said, "but can you
forgive yourself?"

Luke gaped. The
girl was stepping
backwards,
still fixing
him with her
haunting gaze.
Then, before he
could think what
to say, she had

vanished through his bedroom wall.

He shivered. What was happening?

"Ellen! Come back!" But had it been Ellen?

Maybe Luke had just been thinking so deeply about his new song that he had somehow imagined his sister's ghost. But why? It was strange, even frightening.

Luke searched the house. He could hear piano music coming from the sitting room, and in the television room Splodge was still staring at the blank screen, but there was no sign of Ellen. The more Luke thought about her the more he wished he had been nicer to her.

Then he saw the note on the hall table. "Gone to the Unusual Pets Club," it said.

So that was all right then. Or was it?

*

"Right, everyone's here," said Crystal.

"Except for Ellen," said Katy.

"Well, we'll just have to start without her."

Crystal's front room looked like a vet's waiting room. Five children were sitting around with their pets either on their knees or in boxes or cages beside them. Crystal, in the biggest armchair, had to keep moving one hand in front of the other as her hamster Silver ran over them.

"Welcome to the Unusual Pets Club," she said. "We'll take turns to introduce our pets, and then at the end of the meeting we'll vote for the most unusual one. The winner will get this special certificate." She let Katy take Silver while she held out a piece of paper with "Most Unusual Pet of the Week" written on it in big purple letters.

"But won't the same pet just win every week?" asked Martin Booth, whose pet slow-worm was draped contentedly round his neck.

"Not necessarily. New people might join, or someone might get a new pet, or ... well, some pets might just become more unusual. Now, we'll go round in a circle, starting with me." Crystal took Silver back from Katy and explained about his unusual feeding habits. She gave him two pieces of carrot, and sure enough he stuffed them both into his right pouch. Some people clapped, and Crystal smiled smugly.

"You next, Rachel."

Rachel had brought a Siamese cat who was sitting on her knee.

"This is Lapsang," she said. "She's got a very unusual miaow."

"What's unusual about it?" demanded Crystal.

"It's very low. She sounds more like a dog than a cat."

"But all Siamese cats have low voices," said Martin.

"Not as low as Lapsang's," said Rachel.

"Let's hear it then," Crystal ordered.

"Go on, Lapsang – miaow!" Rachel jiggled her legs, disturbing Lapsang's comfortable position. The cat looked offended, jumped off Rachel's lap and stalked silently to the door.

"She'll probably do it later," said Rachel, looking pleadingly at Crystal.

"She'll have to, otherwise you can't stay in the club," said Crystal. She turned to Martin. "Your turn."

"This is Sinclair," said Martin, unwinding his slow-worm from his neck and holding him out. Some of the other children backed away.

"Is he poisonous?" asked Rachel.

Martin gave her a scornful look. "No. He's not a snake. He's a slow-worm. That's a type of lizard – a legless lizard," he said triumphantly.

Everyone looked impressed apart from Crystal, who said, "Well, go on then. Tell us what's unusual about him."

"I've just told you. He hasn't got any legs. Most lizards have legs, don't they?"

"Yes, but slow-worms don't," pointed out Katy. "I think Sinclair would be more unusual if he did have legs."

An argument broke out, with the children taking sides. Crystal had to call the meeting to order.

"We can have the discussion and the vote at the end," she said. "Now, tell us about your guinea pig, Pamina."

"She's got very unusual fur," said Pamina, producing a mangy-looking ginger guinea-pig from a box of straw. "And she's also got a very unusual name – Timbucktoodle-oo."

"Names don't count," Crystal told her. "Tell us what's unusual about the fur."

"Well, you can see," said Pamina. "It's got all these bald patches."

"I don't call that properly unusual," said Crystal. "I'd say she's just got some kind of disease. You ought to take her to the vet. Now, Katy, it's your turn."

But before Katy's stick insect had a chance to show off its dancing talent, there was a ring at the door.

Crystal went to answer it. "Hello, Ellen. You're a bit late," the others heard her say, and the next second a strange-looking dog bounded into the room.

Lapsang's fur stood on end and she at last demonstrated her low-pitched miaow, but this didn't put the new unusual pet off: he made a dash for the cat, who fled across the room and up the curtains.

"Come here, Prince Precious . . . I mean, Splodge!" commanded Ellen, but the dog ignored her. He had spotted Silver the hamster and was leaping up at Crystal. Everyone gasped: for one second it looked as if his jaws had actually closed round the hamster. But a moment later the dog had bounded back to Ellen and Silver was still running about over Crystal's hands.

"Being unusually badly-behaved doesn't count," said Crystal.

"Is Splodge all right?" Katy asked Ellen. "He looks all different – sort of see-through."

"That's his new trick," said Ellen. "He can turn himself into a ghost dog."

Just then the dog gave a growl which was more like the rustle of autumn leaves. He was staring at Sinclair the slow-worm and his ghostly hair was bristling. He backed away, then turned and ran.

"He's gone through the wall!" exclaimed Rachel.

"He couldn't have done," said Crystal.

"He has," said Ellen. "He

can do that. He's a very, very unusual pet."

"There he is — he's looking in through the window!" said Martin.

Lapsang gave another deep miaow, then jumped down from the curtain and slunk into her cat basket.

"Call him back inside, Ellen," said Katy.

"I don't think he'll come if Sinclair is still out," said Ellen.

Martin obligingly put Sinclair into his tank and covered it with his jacket. Meanwhile Rachel put Timbucktoodle-oo back into his box and Crystal shut Silver into his cage. Then Ellen called, "Splodge! Splodge!" and the ghost dog came bounding in through the closed window.

Everyone laughed and clapped. After

that the children had fun getting Ellen's unusual pet to go through various bits of furniture.

"He can even go through people!" boasted Ellen. They all stood in a line, shoulder to shoulder, and sure enough the wildly excited dog jumped through the human wall and back again. After a few goes of this, he leaped through the window again.

"What's he up to now?" said Pamina.

They all crowded to the window. Crystal's little brother was outside, playing football with some friends. The ghost dog was trying to get the ball, but of course his jaws just kept going through it.

"Come back!" Ellen called. The dog turned and gave her a cheeky look, and then he bounded off down the road. She guessed he was going back to his true owner but she didn't tell the others.

"As he's not here any more, no one's allowed to vote for him," said Crystal, but for once the others rose up against her: "That's not fair." "He was at the meeting." "He's so unusual!"

Crystal had to give in. "All right. But remember," and she glared at Ellen, "no one is allowed to vote for their own pet."

The vote took place, and there was no doubt about the winner. Twiglet the stick insect got two votes (from Crystal and Ellen); everyone else voted for the ghost dog.

Rather grumpily, Crystal handed Ellen the certificate. "I hope you realize that the winner has to have the next meeting in their house. It's in the rules," she said.

"That should be fine," said Ellen, "but I don't know if Splodge will be able to do his ghost trick next week. He only does it sometimes."

Everyone except Crystal looked disappointed.

Back home, Ellen had a quick look round for the mirror girl and dog, but there was no sign of them and Mum was calling her to supper.

"Pass the potatoes, please, Ellen," said Luke. "Did you have a good time at the club?" He sounded surprisingly polite.

"Yes, thanks," said Ellen frostily. She still hadn't forgiven him for his behaviour earlier.

"What club?" asked Dad, so Ellen told them a bit about the meeting. She didn't mention Prince Precious Paws. Her family didn't even believe in Mirror-Belle, so she reckoned that a ghost dog would be too much for them to swallow. Instead she pretended that she had just gone along to watch.

"Why didn't you take Splodge with you?" asked Mum.

"He's not unusual enough," Ellen explained. "But maybe I'll be able to teach him a couple of tricks by next week. The meeting's supposed to be here at six o'clock – is that all right?"

Mum agreed, and Luke said, "That's good. You'll have time to watch *Holiday Swap* first."

Ellen gave him a suspicious look. "Why are you being so nice all of a sudden?" she asked. "What's got into you?"

"Just toad-in-the-hole," said Luke,

holding out his plate for a second helping.

"Talking of television," said Dad, "Splodge was behaving very oddly when I was watching the news just now. He kept barking at the television, as if it was going to bite him. And then I noticed that the screen had paw prints on it, as if he'd been attacking it – all very weird."

Ellen smiled. She knew who the paw prints really belonged to. Prince Precious Paws must have gone back through the screen with Mirror-Belle. She felt sorry not to have said goodbye.

"Well, Ellen?" said Luke, breaking into her secret thoughts, and Ellen realized he had been talking to her.

"Sorry, I wasn't concentrating."

"I was just saying," said Luke, "that I've been thinking about Evilton. If you want to borrow him next week, that's fine by me."

About the Author and Illustrator

Julia Donaldson is one of the UK's most popular children's writers. Her award-winning books include *What the Ladybird Heard, The Snail and the Whale* and *The Gruffalo*. She has also written many children's plays and songs, and her sell-out shows based on her books and songs are a huge success. She was the Children's Laureate from 2011 to 2013, campaigning for libraries and for deaf children, and creating a website for teachers called picturebookplays.co.uk. Julia and her husband Malcolm divide their time between Sussex and Edinburgh. You can find out more about Julia at www.juliadonaldson.co.uk.

Lydia Monks studied Illustration at Kingston University, graduating in 1994 with a first-class degree. She is a former winner of the Smarties Bronze Award for *I Wish I Were a Dog* and has illustrated many books by Julia Donaldson. Her illustrations have been widely admired.

Also available

For younger readers

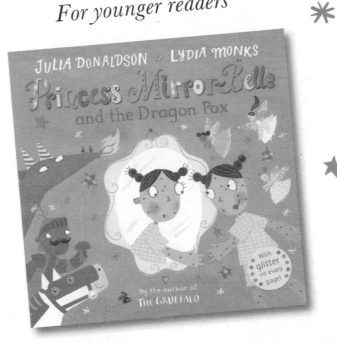

JULIA DONALDSON ❋ LYDIA MONKS

Princess Mirror-Belle
and the Dragon Pox

With
glitter
on every
page!

By the author of
THE GRUFFALO